P9-BYH-482

I PROMISE I'LL FIND YOU

WRITTEN BY HEATHER PATRICIA WARD
ILLUSTRATED BY SHEILA McGRAW

SCHOLASTIC INC.

NEW YORK TORONTO LONDON AUCKLAND SYDNEY

No part of this publication may be reproduced in whole or in part, or stored in
a retrieval system, or transmitted in any form, or by any means, electronic,
mechanical, photocopying, recording, or otherwise, without written permission
of the publisher. For information regarding permission, write to Firefly Books
Ltd., 250 Sparks Avenue, Willowdale, Ontario, Canada, M2H 2S4.

ISBN 0-590-74504-2

Text copyright © 1994 by Heather Patricia Ward.
Illustrations copyright © 1994 by Sheila McGraw.
All rights reserved. Published by Scholastic Inc., 555 Broadway,
New York, NY 10012, by arrangement with Firefly Books Ltd.

12 11 10 9 8 7 6 5 4 3 2   6 7 8 9/9 0 1/0

Printed in the U.S.A.   14

First Scholastic printing, March 1996

I PROMISE
I'LL FIND YOU

This book is dedicated with love
to all of the missing children in the world
and to the memory of Kelly Cook.

If I had a little rowboat,

I'd row across the sea.

I'd row, row, row,

And I'd bring you back to me.

If I had a little airplane,

I'd fly across the sky.

I'd look and look and look for you,

As every day went by.

If I had a little choo-choo train,

I'd chug on down the track.

I'd chug until I found you,

And then I'd bring you back.

If I had a little horsie,

I'd make that horsie run.

He'd run and run and look for you,

Until the day was done.

If I had a little racecar,

I'd race the whole world twice.

I'd find you and I'd keep you,

Oh, that would be so nice.

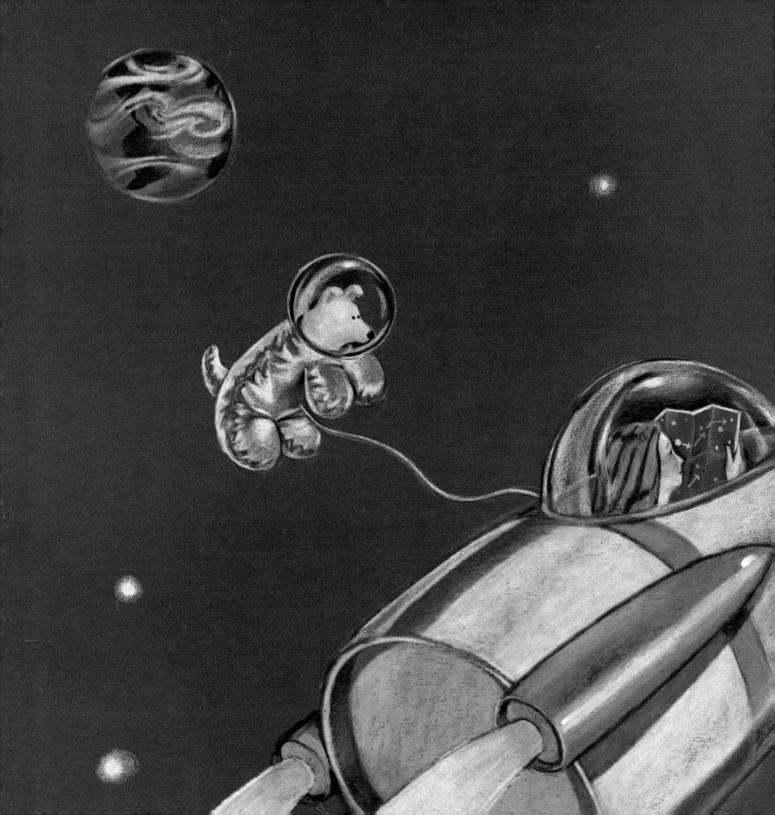

If I had a little rocket ship,

I'd shoot up to the moon.

Oh, that would be the fastest way,

I'd have you really soon.

If I had a little submarine,

I'd go beneath the sea.

I'd scout around to find you,

And hold you next to me.

If I had a little green balloon,

I'd fly all through the air.

I'd pick you up and bring you home,

And you would know I care.

had a little motorbike,

I'd ride across the land.

I'd find you and I'd reach for you,

And you would take my hand.

And if I had no other way,

I'd walk or crawl or run.

I'd search to the very ends of the earth,

For you my precious one.

So remember this my darling,

For it is very true.

If ever you're apart from me,

I'll search till I find you.